I0692508

Charles F. Richardson

The Cross

Charles F. Richardson

The Cross

ISBN/EAN: 9783337255411

Printed in Europe, USA, Canada, Australia, Japan

Cover: Foto ©Andreas Hilbeck / pixelio.de

More available books at **www.hansebooks.com**

HE CROSS.

BY

CHARLES F. RICHARDSON.

———

PHILADELPHIA:

J. B. LIPPINCOTT & CO.

1879.

Copyright, 1879, by CHARLES F. RICHARDSON.

TO MY WIFE.

CONTENTS.

vi   *Contents.*

Repentance.

O CHRIST, who died for men, who died for me,
I fall before thy feet, and cannot see
Aught else beside my grievous sins and thee.

How great my work of evil, thou dost know,
Thou who for me didst grieve and suffer so,
Thou who for me upon the cross didst go.

Whatever thing I see, or hear, or speak,
My sin is still before me ; Lord most meek,
Thy strong and gracious help alone I seek.

That help can put my guilt forever by,
And make me strong when sin again is nigh ;
Forgiving Saviour, give it or I die !

Confession.

WEARY, O Lord, I fall before thy feet,
　And try to tell the number of my sins;
But when the record I would fain repeat,
　My tongue is dumb before its tale begins.

For very shame I dare not speak at all,
　For blinding tears my sad eyes cannot see,
Until, in bitterness of soul, I call,
　"Have mercy, Saviour, heal and pity me."

Then on my head there falls a gracious hand,
　Which takes away the guilt that crushed before;
I hear the Saviour's gentle voice command,
　"Arise forgiven; go and sin no more."

III.

Prayer.

IF, when I kneel to pray,
With eager lips I say:
" Lord, give me all the things that I desire;
Health, wealth, fame, friends, brave heart, religious
    fire,
The power to sway my fellow-men at will,
And strength for mighty works to banish ill;"
    In such a prayer as this
    The blessing I must miss.

    Or if I only dare
    To raise this fainting prayer:
" Thou seest, Lord, that I am poor and weak,
And cannot tell what things I ought to seek;
I therefore do not ask at all, but still
I trust thy bounty all my wants to fill;"
    My lips shall thus grow dumb,
    The blessing shall not come.

    But if I lowly fall,
    And thus in faith I call:
" Through Christ, O Lord, I pray thee give to me
Not what I would, but what seems best to thee,
Of life, of health, of service, and of strength,
Until to thy full joy I come at length;"
    My prayer shall then avail,
    The blessing shall not fail.

IV.

Consecration.

BEHOLD, O Lord, the life thou didst bestow ;
  I offer thee thine own, oh make it thine !
Let soul, and mind, and body purer grow
  Till they be thy life and no longer mine.

For thee my hands would work, my lips would
      speak,
  For thee my ears would hear, my eyes would see ;
Thine are the ways my feet would ever seek ;
  Take me, Lord Christ, and make me like to thee !

v.

Amends.

THINK not your duty done when, sad and tearful,
  Your heart recounts its sins,
And praying God for pardon, weak and fearful
  Its better life begins.

Nor rest content when, braver grown and strongei,
  Your days are sweet and pure,
Because you follow evil ways no longer,
  In Christ's defence secure.

Bethink you then, but not with fruitless rueing,
  That bids the past be still,
Of what your life has wrought to men's undoing,
  By influence for ill.

Go forth, and dare not rest until the morrow,
  But, lest it be too late,
Seek out the hearts whose weight of sin and sorrow
  Through you has grown more great.

Take gifts to all of love and reparation,
  Or if it may not be,
Pray Christ, with ceaseless lips, to send salvation
  Till each chained soul be free.

VI.

Gratitude.

GOOD Lord, I would not thank thee
　With empty thought alone,
My burning words would utter
　The joys my life has known ;
Nor all with sounding praises
　Would I thy love display,
But ever I would offer
　The service of to-day.

I cannot give my Maker
　Rare gifts from wood and field,
For his are all the treasures
　That earth and forest yield ;
Nor yet on smoking altar
　My costly homage pay ;
This sacrifice I offer :
　The service of to-day.

If but a cup of water
　To thirsty lips I bring,
God's eye shall see me render
　Rich tribute to the King ;
From gifts I could not make him
　His face would turn away ;
He asks what I can offer,
　The service of to-day.

VII.

Love.

IF suddenly upon the street
My gracious Saviour I should meet,
And he should say, " As I love thee,
What love hast thou to offer me ?"
Then what could this poor heart of mine
Dare offer to that heart divine ?

His eye would pierce my outward show,
His thought my inmost thought would know ;
And if I said, " I love thee, Lord,"
He would not heed my spoken word,
Because my daily life would tell
If verily I loved him well.

If on the day or in the place
Wherein he met me face to face,
My life could show some kindness done,
Some purpose formed, some work begun
For his dear sake, then it were meet
Love's gift to lay at Jesus' feet.

VIII.

Trust.

WHEN skies are all sweet and sunny,
    And life a long day of spring,
Then trust that the gracious Father
    The fulness of joy shall bring.

When sorrow is added to sorrow,
    And gladness seems far and forgot,
Then trust in the hand that is mighty,
    And the mercy that changeth not.

When the hand of death is upon you,
    And life and love grow dim,
Then trust, for God shall not desert you;
    You die, but you go to him.

When the graves of the dead are opened,
    And the heavens together roll,
Then trust, for your Judge is your Saviour,
    Whose death gave life to your soul.

IX.

Faith.

THREE mocking figures slowly wander by me,
  When falls my weary soul on pain and grief;
And long with every evil art they try me;
  Their names are Doubt, Despair, and Unbelief.

Their scoffing forms my shut eyes still are seeing,
  Their hateful plea, though banished, still I hear,
Until the very weight of life and being
  A greater burden seems than I can bear.

Then Faith appears, and brings her gracious mis-
      sion
  Of utter peace to vexed and storm-tossed minds;
My eyes no longer see with blinded vision,
  My troubled soul a firm reliance finds.

With eager hands I seize on truths immortal,
  And closely press them to my joyous heart;
Strong Faith, still lead me onward to God's portal,
  That from thy gladness I may never part.

X.

𝕴𝖒𝖎𝖙𝖆𝖙𝖎𝖔𝖓.

WHERE shall we find a perfect life whereby
To shape our lives for all eternity?

This man is great and wise; the world reveres him,
    Reveres, but cannot love his heart of stone;
And so it dares not follow, though it fears him,
    But bids him walk his mountain path alone.

That man is good and gentle; all men love him,
    Yet dare not ask his feeble arm for aid;
The world's best work is ever far above him,
    He shrinks beneath the storm-capped mountain's
        shade.

O loveless strength! O strengthless love! the Master
    Whose life shall shape our lives is not as thou;
Sweet Friend in peace, strong Saviour in disaster,
    Our heart of hearts enfolds thine image now!

Be Christ's the fair and perfect life whereby
We shape our lives for all eternity.

XI.

Service.

IF life were naught but living,
  And death were only death,
Would life be worth the giving,
  Would men thank God for breath ?

Ah no ! for sweeter, dearer,
  To toil, and pray, and fast,
If so the Lord draw nearer,
  And bring his peace at last.

Who follows him, sees mercies
  In every bitter pain ;
Who follows not, finds curses
  Beneath all worldly gain.

XII.

Diligence.

IF but at morn unto your God you go,
   And seek his aid for toils not yet begun,
That neither haste nor rest your hands may know
   Until each daily duty well be done;

If but at noon your zeal fade not away,
   And heart and hand their steadfast work pursue,
In cheery confidence that all the day
   New strength shall come for every labor new;

If but at night you lay your task aside,
   Nor grieve lest in God's sight it seem but small,
Content to wait, whatever may betide,
   For God in his good time shall finish all;

Then days shall wax to months, and months to
      years,
   And years make up a life that God shall own;
And when the messenger of Death appears
   His hand shall bring a laurel from the Throne.

XIII.

Perseverance.

Two voices follow me,
  They both are always near ;
When I am weak and cowardly
  The first falls on my ear,
But whether I am weak or brave
  The second voice I hear.

Thus loudly cries the first :
  " In vain your strength you spend ;
The way is long, the toil is hard,
  You cannot see the end ;
No longer struggle up the steep ;
  Come hither, rest you, friend."

The second voice, more sweet,
  Thus whispers soft and low :
" What though the road seem rough and long,
  Its every step I know,
And I will help you all the while ;
  Friend, bravely onward go."

This is the voice, O Lord,
  That I will ever heed,
Thine be the rule of all my life,
  In thought, and word, and deed ;
Though dark and distant be the path,
  I follow, do thou lead.

XIV.

𝔖𝔱𝔯𝔢𝔫𝔤𝔱𝔥.

THE power that shaped the everlasting hills
    Can nerve with ghostly strength the Christian's
        arm,
For God himself his servants' hope fulfils,
    And bids them onward go, secure from harm.

If he defend us not, our strength shall fail,
    Though set about with all that man can give,
But helped by God, the weakest shall not quail,
    The fainting shall arise, the dead shall live.

Nor need we wait for some great crucial day
    Before we seek in God's defence to stand;
He guides the sweeping planets on their way,
    But leads his little children by the hand.

xv.

Courage.

WE have chosen to follow the crucified Lord
Though he lead us through dangers of fire and of
     sword ;
We know not what perils await us before,
But the tents we have left we will enter no more.

Our hearts burn within us, for Christ is our guide,
His courage our courage, we fight by his side ;
Though we faint or we fall, we go on to the end,
The wrong to destroy and the right to defend.

Thus battle we ever for Christ and the cross,
No step we take backward, no toil we count loss ;
And bravest we struggle when darkest the day,
For the hand of our Leader still points us the way.

XVI.

Prudence.

THE way of life is narrow,
  It passes through the night,
Thick branches seek to hide it,
  And clouds refuse it light;
But far ahead is glowing
  The morning's beacon bright.

Who watches with clear vision
  That ever-guiding ray,
Nor turns with idle longing
  To look beside the way,
Shall thread the narrow footpath
  And greet the dawning day.

But if he cease his watching,
  And fain would stop to hear
Strange sounds from out the darkness
  That sweetly greet his ear,
His wandering foot shall stumble
  On dangers hiding near.

The prudent heart is bravest,
  Nor fears the braggart's blame,
It dares to do its duty,
  But shuns the zealot's shame;
No wilder wars pursuing,
  It battles in Christ's name.

XVII.

Temperance.

GOD gives to man five wits:
To see, to hear, to smell, to touch, to taste;
He gives them all to use, but none to waste;
    To each its rule he fits.

Man may not use his eyes
To turn with longing gaze on distant fields
Whose evil soil malignant fruitage yields,
    Though fair its blossoms rise.

Nor may his eager lips,
All careless of the serpent in the vine,
Receive the luring cup of Circe's wine,
    That poisons him who sips.

But he whose every sense
Is made a gate where nought can enter in
That bears upon its front one mark of sin,
    Shall have God's own defence.

It is the Holy Ghost
Who takes man's body for his temple fair;
And he who guards it with most constant care
    Shall please its Tenant best.

XVIII.

Truth:

THERE stands a Guide before me
　Who comes in Jesus' name;
A star shines in her forehead,
　She bears a sword of flame.

Her eyes look through and through me,
　They burn with endless youth,
Her hand points ever onward;
　It is the hand of Truth.

I know not where she goeth,
　But I must follow, too,
In pleasant paths or thorny,
　The distant journey through.

She shuns the ways I trusted,
　And where I dared not go
She bids me enter fearless,
　God's treasures there to know.

Thus all along life's pathway
　Truth shows the upward way,
Until her guidance brings me
　To God's eternal day.

XIX.

Justice.

A HUNDRED noble wishes fill my heart,
   I long to help each soul in need of aid ;
In all good works my zeal would have its part,
   Before no weight of toil it stands afraid.

But noble wishes are not noble deeds,
   And he does least who seeks to do the whole ;
Who works the best, his simplest duties heeds,
   Who moves the world, first moves a single soul.

Then go, my heart, thy plainest work begin,
   Do first not what thou canst, but what thou must ;
Build not upon a corner-stone of sin,
   Nor seek great works until thou first be just.

XX.

Charity.

WHATEVER be the sin that grieves my sight,
Whatever wrong I struggle to make right,
On sin and wrong more grievous I must fall,
If charity I show not first of all ;
Shall God or man have charity for me
When I, poor soul, refuse it unto thee ?

But if, when sin and woe I strive to heal,
The grace of charity I soonest feel,
Then Christ's rebuke, not mine, my life shall show,
For he shall walk beside me where I go,
And God and men have charity for me,
Since I, poor soul, bestow it upon thee.

XXI.

Comfort.

A SINGLE word is a little thing,
  But a soul may be dying before your eyes
For lack of the comfort a word may bring,
  With its welcome help and its sweet surprise.

A kindly look costs nothing at all,
  But a heart may be starving for just one glance
That shall show by the eyelid's tender fall
  The help of a pitying countenance.

It is easy enough to bend the ear
  To catch some tale of sore distress ;
But men may be fainting beside us here,
  For longing to share their weariness.

These gifts nor silver nor gold may buy,
  Nor the wealth of the richest of men bestow,
But the comfort of word, or ear, or eye
  The poorest may offer wherever he go.

XXII.

𝔥𝔢𝔩𝔭.

THE world is full of labor,
   It toils in weariness;
You cannot bear its burden,
   But you can make it less.

A little child is trying
   To lift a heavy load;
Go, help the helpless toiler
   Along the weary road.

A poor old friendless woman
   Is tottering on alone;
Her trembling strength has failed her;
   Go, offer her your own.

Though little be each action,
   Its heart the Lord shall see;
And his shall be the witness:
   "Ye did it unto me."

Patience.

IF, when you labor all the day,
You see its minutes slip away
With joy unfound, with work undone,
And hope descending with the sun,

Then cheerily lie down to rest;
The longest work shall be the best;
And when the morrow greets your eyes,
With strong and patient heart arise.

For Patience, stern and leaden-eyed,
Looks far where future joys abide;
Nor sees short sadness at her feet,
For sight of triumph long and sweet.

XXIV.

𝕳𝖔𝖕𝖊.

WHEN thick on our hearts fall the clouds of the
    night,
And grief and distress banish joy from our sight,
Though deep in the darkness of sorrow we grope,
We bear in our bosoms the promise of hope.

When woe, sin, and death whisper naught but
    despair,
And there fades from our lips the sweet purpose of
    prayer,
Then back to our Father does hope lead the way,
And fair in the gloom shines the promise of day.

Or if God in his love grant us gladness and peace,
Think not that the gifts of his bounty shall cease;
Still onward points hope, for God's future is long,
To the wise shall come wisdom, and strength to
        the strong.

XXV.

𝔓urity.

WE cannot reach thy kingdom, Lord,
  Nor look to heaven's door,
Until with childhood's purity
  Our hearts grow bright once more.

The pure in heart their God shall see,
  Of such his kingdom is,
And childlike ears alone can hear
  The heavenly harmonies.

The gentle word, the guileless mind,
  The trustful soul are theirs,
The little children of the Lord,
  Whose lily life he shares.

XXVI.

Humility.

HUMILITY is not to say
   " I know that I am less than God,"
Nor yet with meekness to obey
   The law's decree, the ruler's rod.

The humble heart is quick to see
   A nobler heart in any breast;
And knows it not, although it be
   Itself more great than all the rest.

No jot of wisdom shall it miss,
   It knows its ignorance so well;
The whole wide world its teacher is,
   To it the heavens their secrets tell.

It sees, when others blind their eyes;
   It builds, when all men overthrow;
And so at length, in strange surprise,
   It reigns where fallen pride lies low.

XXVII.

Sacrifice.

SHORT is the lesson the Master hath taught us,
  Plain is its meaning, that all men may know;
Close in your heart hide the gift that he brought us,
  Out in your life let its influence go.

This is the word that he brought us from heaven :
  Give unto others the things you count dear :
Not for yourself be the life you are given ;
  Not all your own be your happiness here.

Speed thee to labor, and sorrow, and trial,
  Strong be the heart that is weary and sore ;
Welcome be hate, and neglect, and denial,
  If but the Master hath known them before.

So shall your heritage all be immortal,
  Thieves shall not steal it, nor canker destroy ;
Glimpses of glory shall brighten death's portal,
  Sorrow and sacrifice rise into joy.

XXVIII.

𝔓𝔢𝔞𝔠𝔢.

IF sin be in the heart,
The fairest sky is foul, and sad the summer weather,
The eye no longer sees the lambs at play together,
The dull ear cannot hear the birds that sing so
　　sweetly,
And all the joy of God's good earth is gone com-
　　pletely,
　　　　If sin be in the heart.

If peace be in the heart,
The wildest winter storm is full of solemn beauty,
The midnight lightning flash but shows the path of
　　duty,
Each living creature tells some new and joyous
　　story,
The very trees and stones all catch a ray of glory,
　　　　If peace be in the heart.

XXIX.

Wisdom.

A CANDLE in the night
But little space makes bright ;
And when the skylark sings
He soars on fading wings.

Thus wisdom may not see
The things that distant be,
Nor may its eager ear
The world's far secrets hear.

But God exists ; what more
Lies hid in learned lore?
My duty well I know ;
Has life aught else to show?

God's works and ways I see,
God's wisdom teaches me ;
I seek no other guide
If He be at my side.

xxx.

Worship.

BRAVE spirit, that will brook no intervention,
    But thus alone before thy God dost stand,
Content if he but see thy heart's intention,—
    Why spurn the suppliant knee and outstretched
        hand ?

Sweet soul, that kneelest in the solemn glory
    Of yon cathedral altar, while the prayer
Of priest or bishop tells thine own heart's story,—
    Why think that they alone heaven's keys may
        bear ?

Man worships with the heart; for wheresoever
    One burning pulse of heartfelt homage stirs,
There God shall straightway find his own, and
        never,
    In church or desert, miss his worshippers.

XXXI.

𝔓raise.

I PRAISE thee, God the Father, for this good gift of
    life,
Else I had never known the joy that brightens
    Christian strife.

I praise thee, Christ the Saviour, for all thine earthly
    woe ;
Hadst thou not grieved and died for me, I had not
    loved thee so.

I praise thee, Holy Spirit, thy grace hath entered
    in ;
Until thy light fell on my heart, I could not see my
    sin.

I praise thee, blessed Trinity, Creator, Saviour,
    Guide ;
O let the thanks that fill my soul forever there
    abide !

XXXII.

Joy.

A SENSE of joy is not enough;
  The Christian's face should shine
As with a heavenly radiance
  Of happiness divine.

Mere looks of joy are not enough;
  The Christian's words should tell
To every ear that God is good,
  And loves his creatures well.

Bright words of joy are not enough;
  The Christian's life should show
The gladness springing in his heart,
  That all its source may know.

A joyful life is not enough;
  The Christian's death should be
A gladsome passing through the gate
  Of immortality.

XXXIII.

Triumph.

OUR war is full of danger,
  Its fight is fierce and long,
Temptations crowd before us,
  Behind are sin and wrong ;
But through the smoke of conflict
  We see the victor's palm,
And catch, beyond the struggle,
  A glimpse of holy calm.

There stands the sacred city,
  Aflame in golden light ;
There Jesus waits in glory
  To greet each faithful knight ;
There throngs of saints and angels
  Lift up their glad acclaim :
" These victors won their crowning,
  They conquered in His name."

Then, brothers, speed we onward,
  This world shall waste away,
Its kings and kingdoms perish,
  Its night-time follow day ;
Though stars and suns shall crumble,
  And time's procession cease,
We seek our home in heaven,
  The long abode of peace.

www.ingramcontent.com/pod-product-compliance
Lightning Source LLC
Chambersburg PA
CBHW030914260626
47169CB00008B/2848